PUFFIN BOOKS

THE CHRISTMASAURUS CRACKER

THE CHRISTMASAURUS CRACKER

TOM FLETCHER

Illustrations by Shane Devries

PUFFIN

PUFFIN BOOKS

UK | USA | Canada | Ireland | Australia
India | New Zealand | South Africa

Puffin Books is part of the Penguin Random House group of companies
whose addresses can be found at global.penguinrandomhouse.com.

www.penguin.co.uk   www.puffin.co.uk   www.ladybird.co.uk

Penguin
Random House
UK

First published 2022
001

Please supervise children in the kitchen at all times and always use appropriate
kitchen safety measures. The recipes in this book may not be suitable for those with
food allergies or intolerances. Please check the recipes carefully for the presence of
any ingredients or substances that may cause an adverse reaction if consumed by
those with any food allergy or intolerance. The recipes have not been formally tested
and the publisher accepts no responsibility or liability for them.

Printed in Great Britain by Clays Ltd, Elcograf S.p.A.

The authorized representative in the EEA is Penguin Random House Ireland,
Morrison Chambers, 32 Nassau Street, Dublin D02 YH68

A CIP catalogue record for this book is available from the British Library

ISBN: 978-0-241-62445-6

All correspondence to:
Puffin Books, Penguin Random House Children's
One Embassy Gardens, 8 Viaduct Gardens, London SW11 7BW

To everyone who loves Christmas!

CONTENTS

CRUMPET EVE

'Crumpets are tasty,
Crumpets are yum,
They go in your mouth
And come out of your . . .'

Oh, hi! It's your favourite elf here. No, not Sprout, you cheeky sausage! It's me – Spudcheeks, of course! You know, the one with the big moustache who toasts the crumpets.

Now, I know what you're thinking: *Why aren't you speaking in elf-rhyme?* Well, the truth is that

2

we don't always speak in rhyme. We mostly just do that because it annoys the jingles out of Santa, and there's nothing funnier than seeing a man who's dressed from head to toe in red turn red in the face. Don't tell him, though!

My role up here in the NPSR – that's the North Pole Snow Ranch – isn't just toasting crumpets (and eating them). No, no, no – my official title is Chief Checker of Crumpet Conditions. Which is a fancy-pants way of saying that I'm responsible for looking after the most important part of any elf Christmas . . .

CRUMPETS!

And, if you've been paying attention to the rest of this book, you'll know that we elves LOVE crumpets!

It's a tricky job, but some-elf has to do it!

Oh, I remember one year when everything nearly went butterside-down. Here's what happened:

It was the last day of November and Sizzlewhisk, the baking elf, had just taken the last batch of warm

Christmas crumpets out of the oven. She was a feisty elf, that Sizzlewhisk, with hair the colour of baked dough, which she kept tied in two wrap-around plaits on either side of her head, making her look as though her freckled face were sandwiched between two delicious pastries.

'That's it – I'm all done. Don't eat 'em all at once. See you next year!' she chirped before twisting her floury orange apron around herself and disappearing in a cloud of crumbs. No one knew where she vanished to, but Sizzlewhisk magically reappeared in the NPSR on the last day of November each year to bake our supply of Christmas crumpets to get us through the busy season. That's why we call that day **Crumpet Eve!**

No one baked them like Sizzlewhisk. Fluffy but firm. Airy but filling. The perfect munch for hard-working North Pole elves.

That night, piles and piles of her fluffiest,

crumbliest, scrummiest crumpets were cooling in the pantry . . . So, before heading to bed, I thought I'd go and tuck the crumpets in. And perhaps sing them a little lullaby – I am Chief Checker of Crumpet Conditions, after all. If you're thinking that I was going to go and help myself to a cheeky, sneaky, late-night crumpet snack, you are totally wrong. OK, I might have had a teensy nibble if it weren't for, well, you'll see . . .

When I arrived, I was surprised to find the pantry door **WIDE OPEN**, and there was a strange snoring sound coming from within.

It wasn't an elf snore, nor was it Santa's rumbling snore.

'Who's there?' I called into the darkness, but the reply was just more strange snoring. I peeked inside and to my surprise came face to face with a sleeping blue dinosaur!

'Chrissy! You scared the Kringles out of me, you big wallybags!' I squeaked, jumping with fright.

The Christmasaurus woke up, startled.

'What in the North Pole is that around your mouth?' I asked, noticing some strange fluffy crumbs on his sparkly blue scales.

My little elf heart sank as I realized what they were.

'Crumpet crumbs!' I gasped. 'Have you been eating Sizzlewhisk's crumpets?!'

The Christmasaurus nodded his head sheepishly and stepped aside, revealing the most frightening thing I've ever seen. The thought of it still gives me the shivers. It was the sight of . . .

NO CRUMPETS!

'How? Who? Why? When? But? If? What?
Did you really eat the lot?
From scaly head to sparkly toe,
You're so full of crumpet dough
That if I were to X-ray you
I'd just see crumpets, through and through!
Us elves need crumpets every day:
Without them we'll just fade away.
For elves there's nothing more nutritious –
No crumpets means there'll be
NO CHRISTMAS!
So, you and I must put this right,
Not tomorrow. Now, tonight!'

I hopped on to Chrissy's scaly blue back and
we raced to the Snow Ranch kitchen. While Santa
and my fellow elves slept, I quietly whipped out
the large mixing bowl and a whisk.

'Let me think. Flour, water . . . What else goes
into crumpets?' I whispered.

Chrissy shrugged.

'Well, don't look at me like that! I just CHECK the crumpets – I don't bake them!' I said as my dinosaur companion raised an icy eyebrow in my direction, and then I opened the enormous refrigerator.

'Christmas pudding?
Put it in!

Mince pie?
In it flies!

Broccoli?
Probably!

Cabbage and cress?
Yes, yes, yes!

Brussels sprouts?
. . . Leave those out.'

I chanted as we threw all the ingredients (minus the sprouts) into the bowl.

A few hours later our broccoli, cabbage, mince pie, Christmas pudding-flavoured crumpets were done. Chrissy took the first bite and I saw his icy blue face turn green before he spat out the lot.

'Oh, this is useless! The elves can't dig toys without crumpets and there's barely even a crumb left to go around!' I cried. Suddenly I felt the Christmasaurus hoist me up on to his back again.

Chrissy had an idea!

In a blue flash, we were stood next to the most magical vehicle in the whole world, Santa's sleigh.

'By jingles, of course! We can use the sleigh to fly and pick up some fresh crumpets. We'll be back here before you can say *jingle bells*,' I said, scrambling into the enormous red sleigh.

The Christmasaurus slipped into his flying harness, let out a roar and leaped into a gallop.

I tumbled to the back of the sleigh as we floated off the floor, through the open ceiling and into the snowy sky.

We soared across the stars on our covert crumpet crusade. I held on as tightly as I could with my three elf fingers while the Christmasaurus giddily galloped along the Northern Lights.

Before long we were crossing oceans and cities on our search for baked perfection – then suddenly my twisty moustache started twitching.

'Oooh, I think I might have sniffed a scent! Take us down, Chrissy!' I called, and the Christmasaurus spiralled down towards a twinkly city with a castle in the middle.

'Scotland?' I asked, hearing the merry sound of bagpipes from below.

The Christmasaurus nodded, recognizing it having pulled Santa's sleigh around the world many times.

We landed on a roof above a high street.

'This is it!' I said, noticing the increasingly excitable twitches from the moustache under my honker. 'There must be crumpets here!'

I nipped down the nearest chimney and followed my twitching moustache to a round tin in the kitchen. I grabbed it and whizzed back up to the sleigh to inspect what was inside.

'It smells like a crumpet, but it doesn't really look like one!' I said, looking at the long flat dough.

I quickly fired up the portable crumpet oven (Santa always keeps one in his sleigh) and toasted it so we could each have a nibble.

'Tasty!' I said, and the Christmasaurus agreed, 'but it's not **Sizzlewhisk** tasty!'

And with that we popped the tin of funny non-crumpets back down the chimney, then shot back into the sky.

We swished over the clouds for only a few moments before my moustache started twitching yet again.

'Down we go, Chrissy!' I called, and we dived towards the smell. The small village below had cobbled streets with a light dusting of snow. 'That one!' I said, pointing at the house with a scrummy smell of baked yumminess wafting from its chimney.

We landed silently and I slipped down into the house, quieter than a ninja-Santa.

'The galettes are ready,' a dear old lady said in another language. Luckily for me, the sleigh has a portable translator that allows you to understand anything that is said in the house below it. It was an optional extra, but Santa thought it might be useful.

I hid behind the Christmas tree as her family wandered into the kitchen and the old lady handed out a strange, waffly-looking biscuit, or was it a biscuity-looking waffle? I wasn't sure, but the second she put the plate down I slipped one from the pile and zoomed back up the chimney.

'It's called a *galette*,' I explained as Chrissy sniffed the waffle-biscuit excitedly. 'It's good . . . but it's not Sizzlewhisk good.'

Whoosh!

We were off again, back on our quest for the best crumpets on Earth.

Next stop was a pancake house in California: yummy, but not Sizzlewhisk yummy.

We sampled crepes in Calais: warm, but not Sizzlewhisk warm.

Chrissy chomped four whole panettoni in Italy: fluffy, but not Sizzlewhisk fluffy.

'It's no use, Chrissy! We've been from one corner of the globe to the other, and tasted pastries and pancakes, brioche and biscuits, doughnuts and doughballs, but they're not a pinch on our Christmas crumpets.' I sighed heavily as we sailed through the sky. 'We're going to have to go back empty-handed and . . .'

Just then my moustache twitched.

'Oh!'

This twitch was different. Stronger, more excited than the others, like it was tugging me towards crumpets.

'Dive, Chrissy, **DIVE!**'

The Christmasaurus tucked his scaly legs in and we raced down towards the wafting waves of wonderful baking.

'Bolton?' I said, glancing at a passing street sign as we raced towards a glorious building up ahead.

We circled the large, steaming chimneys and set the sleigh down on the gigantic roof.

'This is the biggest bakery I've ever seen!' I shouted into the seemingly bottomless chimney.

The Christmasaurus slid out of his harness and we both leaped down the chimney together.

We fell and fell and fell for what felt like forever.

'This is the deepest chimney I've ever seen!' I yelled before we finally landed in a basket of soft, fluffy pillows.

'Wow!' I gasped.

WOW, WOW, WOW . . .

my echo replied from the brilliant bakery before us. There must have been a billion loaves of bread bustling along a conveyor belt, heading towards bright orange crates.

'Lucky these pillows were here to break our fall, eh, Chrissy!' I said, feeling the fluffiness beneath my bottom, but then I noticed something in Chrissy's mouth. 'Don't eat the pill-oh . . . CRUMPETS!' I gasped.

'Fluffy, airy, thick, soft crumpets!' I said, inspecting the circular discs of deliciousness beneath me. 'Why, these crumpets are so good they're almost –'

'I don't believe my eyeballs!' interrupted a familiar, warm voice.

'**SIZZLEWHISK!**' I cried, leaping off the pile of crumpets with joy at seeing the baking elf. 'What are you doing here?'

'I should ask you the same question. What's a North Pole elf and a dinosaur doing in Bolton?' Sizzlewhisk asked, leaning on a giant rolling pin and looking a bit cross that Chrissy was still sitting on her freshly baked batch of crumpets.

'Crumpets!'
I blurted.
'We need more crumpets – it's an emergency!'

'MORE? But I only just baked your Christmas supply! Where on earth have they all gone?'

The Christmasaurus hung his head in shame.

'I see,' said Sizzlewhisk with a sigh. 'Well, dinosaurs do have big appetites, I suppose. Santa will have to place a bigger order next year.'

'*Next year?* But the North Pole elves can't
work without crumpets. If we go back
empty-handed, Christmas is done for!'
I said in a wobbly voice.

There was a pause while Sizzlewhisk thought
about what to do.

'Well, there's only one thing for it,' she said,
throwing something orange at me.

'What's this?' I asked, catching the piece of
material.

'It's an apron for you. You want crumpets?
You'd better get baking! You too, you big
crumpet thief,' she said, tying another apron
around Chrissy's icy mane.

Chrissy and I followed Sizzlewhisk through the
magical bakery, past the pots and pans, the ovens
and rollers. It was like the North Pole Snow Ranch,
but instead of toys there was dough!

Sizzlewhisk called out the ingredients while

Chrissy and I mixed them all together. We followed every instruction she gave us and before we knew it there was an enormous batch of the freshest, warmest, fluffiest Christmas crumpets baking in the ovens.

'Very nice,' she said, admiring our baking. 'Couldn't have done it better myself!'

'So, is this where you work?' I asked, looking around at the bakery.

'Only part-time. The humans are good bakers, but it takes an elf to make proper crumpets. That's why these taste the best! I do the night shift when no one else is around,' Sizzlewhisk said with a wink. 'Don't tell the humans, though.' She pulled one of our crumpets out to check. **All done!**

We loaded the sleigh until it was overflowing with crumpets.

'Thanks a lot, Sizzlewhisk,' I said, giving my fellow elf a hug.

'That's OK. Just promise me you won't

eat them all this time!' she said, giving Chrissy a stroke and a little nibble on a buttery crumpet for the flight home.

'Now, you'd better get going if you want to be back before Santa wakes up.'

And, with that command from Sizzlewhisk, the Christmasaurus galloped across the bakery roof and rocketed into the air, pulling the heavy load of crumpets up into the Bolton sky.

'See you next year!' I called as we whizzed through the clouds.

We made it home just in time for breakfast.

'These are the freshest crumpets I've ever tasted!' munched Sparklefoot.

'Sizzlewhisk has outdone herself this year,' gobbled Starlump.

'Oh yes! I could dig up toys for days with these crumbly treats,' chomped Snowcrumb.

'How does she get them this good?' slurped Sprout, with butter dripping down his beard.

Chrissy and I stared around the room as everyone enjoyed their first Christmas crumpets.

'No one bakes crumpets quite like Sizzlewhisk,' I said with a smile and a wink that only the Christmasaurus saw.

THE END

CHRISTMAS FACTS FROM THE TRUNDLES

Oh, hello!
I'm William Trundle.

Here's something you should know about me . . .

I love Christmas!

And so does my dad, Bob Trundle. In fact, he loves Christmas **SOOOOOO** much, he keeps a secret Christmas tree hidden inside his wardrobe all-year round. (And it's fully decorated.) Dad loves Christmas so much that he taught me some of his favourite Christmas facts! Would you like to know them too? **OK!**

Did you know that . . .

1   **Santa Claus** hasn't always worn red! He has also worn green, purple and blue. It wasn't until the 1930s, when artist Haddon Sundblom decided to paint Santa dressed up in red for a Coca-Cola Christmas advert, that the colour stuck. I'm very glad it did, because red definitely suits him!

2   'Jingle Bells' was the first song to be played in **space!** On 16 December 1965, it was played by the crew of NASA's Gemini 6A space flight. 'Jingle Bells' even holds a Guinness World Record for being the first song to be played outside our atmosphere. (As far as we know . . .)

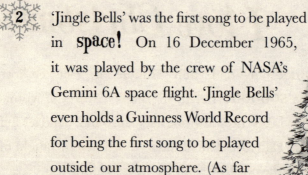

3 **Christmas trees** haven't always been around! Before Queen Victoria, who was queen over a hundred years ago, most people didn't have a Christmas tree in the UK. When she married Prince Albert, who was German, a newspaper published a drawing of the royal family celebrating around a decorated tree. It was a tradition that Prince Albert had brought over to England from Germany. Over time, more and more families decided to copy the idea!

4 **Christmas crackers** are a Victorian invention too. When Tom Smith, a sweet-maker from London, visited Paris in 1848, he noticed packages of sugared almonds wrapped in twists of paper for sale. They gave him the idea for the very first Christmas cracker: small packages full of sweets that would burst apart when you pulled them!

5 **Christmas lights** came a little bit later. In 1882 – just three years after inventor Thomas Edison came up with the light bulb – one of his friends, Edward Johnson, decorated his tree with the very first string of Christmas lights.

6 There are more than **ONE THOUSAND** types of mistletoe!

7 There's an official **Christmas Jumper Day** every year. (It's my dad's favourite day of the year after Christmas Day – even though he wears Christmas jumpers all-year round.) There are even competitions for the most hideous jumper!

8 If you gave someone all the gifts from the **'Twelve Days of Christmas'** – a partridge in a pear tree right the way up to twelve lords a-leaping – that would be three hundred and sixty-four presents. Almost enough for one for every day of the year!

9 The smallest fully-grown dinosaur fossil ever discovered is the **lesothosaurus** – it's only the size of a chicken.

Oh, wait. That's a **dinosaur** fact! Did I mention I also **REALLY** love dinosaurs?!

10 Traditionally, Santa has **nine reindeer**: Dasher, Dancer, Prancer, Vixen, Comet, Cupid, Donner, Blitzen and Rudolph. The first eight names came from 'Twas the Night Before Christmas', a poem by Clement Clarke Moore from 1823. Rudolph, however, first appeared over a hundred years later in a 1939 story – *Rudolph the Red-nosed Reindeer* by Robert L. May.

'Every second
away from
LAST CHRISTMAS
is one second CLOSER
TO THE NEXT.'

STOCKING SURPRISE

Here's a fun memory game you can play with your family at Christmas.

Find a **blank piece of paper** and trace round the stocking shape on the opposite page. Then grab your **colouring pencils** and fill your stocking with lots of presents! You can choose anything: books, toys, Christmas jumpers, a ride on Santa's sleigh – even your very own Christmasaurus. The more presents, the trickier the game will be . . .

Once you're finished, ask your family to take a quick look at the stocking – no more than five seconds. Then turn over your picture so they can't see it any more.

Now test your family and see how many of your presents they can remember!

SNOWCRUMB'S BEST FESTIVE RECIPES

Here are some of Snowcrumb the elf's scrummiest festive treats. Before you begin baking, please make sure you ask a grown-up for permission and help – especially with using hot frying pans and the oven.

SNOWCRUMB'S SUPER-SECRET
CRUMPET RECIPE

Ingredients

Makes 6 mouth-watering crumpets

150 g plain white flour

200 ml water

½ tsp salt

1 tsp dried yeast

½ tsp sugar

1 tsp baking powder

Snowcrumb's steps

1 Wash your hands really well with water and lots of soap.

2 Add the flour, water and salt to a mixing bowl and **WHISK, WHISK, WHISK** for around 5 minutes. (Make sure you use a generous-sized bowl as the mixture is going to **GET BIGGER!**)

3 In a separate bowl, mix a splash of water into the dried yeast. Then add sugar, baking powder and the yeast mixture to your big mixing bowl. Next, mix for another 30 seconds until you have a smooth batter.

31

4   Cover your mixing bowl and put it in a warm place for 15 minutes to settle.

5   With the permission and help of a grown-up, place a greased metal biscuit cutter in the middle of a non-stick frying pan.

6   Preheat the frying pan on a hob on a medium-high heat setting.

7   Give your batter one final big **STIR, STIR, STIR** to remove any large air bubbles.

8   Use a ladle to drop batter into the cutter in the frying pan.

9   Wait about 4 minutes, then carefully lift the cutter away from the crumpet. If the top still looks a bit under-baked, flip the crumpet over in the pan for a few seconds.

10   Remove your cooked crumpet from the pan and allow it to cool.

11   Repeat steps 8 to 10 until you've used up the rest of the batter.

12   Toast your crumpets and add your favourite topping before tucking in! **YUM!**

JINGLE-BELL
GINGERBREAD

Gingerbread has been baked around the world for **YEARS** and **YEARS** and **YEARS!** It can be traced back as far as the Ancient Greeks and Egyptians. Gingerbread was a popular treat at medieval festivals across Europe, and now it's seen as the perfect Christmas treat around the world!

Here are some **GINGERBREAD FACTS** you might not know.

- Gingerbread houses were first created in Germany, where they became popular after the Brothers Grimm published their famous story 'Hansel and Gretel'.
- Queen Elizabeth I was a big gingerbread fan, and to celebrate important guests she would present them with gingerbread portraits of themselves!

- In one tradition from Sweden, you can put a piece of gingerbread in your palm and make a wish. Then break the gingerbread with your other hand. If it breaks into three, your wish is granted!
- The world's largest gingerbread house was baked and built in Texas, USA, in 2013. It was big enough to fit a family of five inside and holds a Guinness World Record.
- In Europe, gingerbread was once used as a cure for indigestion and upset stomachs!

Ingredients

Makes 20 gingerbread biscuits

350 g plain flour, plus a sprinkle extra for dusting

2 tsp ground ginger

1 tsp ground cinnamon

1 tsp bicarbonate of soda

125 g butter

175 g brown sugar

1 large egg

4 tbsp golden syrup

Icing in your
favourite colours

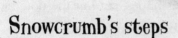

Snowcrumb's steps

1 Wash your hands really well with water and lots of soap.

2 With the permission and help of a grown-up, preheat the oven to 180 degrees Celsius.

3 Line two baking trays with greaseproof paper.

4 With the help of a grown-up, add the flour, ginger, cinnamon, baking soda and butter to a food processor, then **WHIZZ, WHIZZ, WHIZZ** until you have a breadcrumb-like mixture.

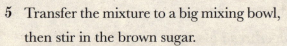

5   Transfer the mixture to a big mixing bowl, then stir in the brown sugar.

6   Beat the egg and golden syrup together in a separate bowl, and then add to the mixing bowl, stirring until everything clumps together.

7   Lightly dust a clean surface with flour and then tip your mixture out on to the floured surface. Knead the mixture until smooth, wrap in cling film, and leave to chill in the fridge for 15 minutes. You can sing your favourite Christmas songs while you wait!

8   Lightly dust your surface again and roll out the chilled dough, until it is about half a centimetre thick.

9   Using cutters in your chosen shapes, cut out the dough and place carefully on the baking trays. Make sure to leave a gap between each biscuit!

10 With the help of a grown-up, bake the biscuits in the oven for 12–15 minutes, or until they are a lovely golden-brown colour. Leave to cool on the tray for 10 minutes, and then move them on to a wire rack to finish cooling.

11 When the biscuits are completely cool, it's time to decorate! Get creative with your coloured icing and decorate your very own gingerbread treats.

CHRISTMASAURUS
HOT CHOCOLATE

The perfect treat to drink on Christmas Eve as you wait for Santa to arrive . . .

Ingredients

250 ml milk (use any milk you like: it can be dairy, almond, oat, soy or another kind)

1 tbsp cocoa powder

4 tbsp maple syrup

1 drop vanilla extract

A pinch of cinnamon

Snowcrumb's steps

1   Wash your hands really well with water and lots of soap.

2   Add all the ingredients to a small saucepan.

3   Gently whisk over a medium heat until steaming and all the ingredients are combined, and your mixture just starts to boil.

4   Pour into a mug and serve with your favourite toppings, like whipped cream and big fluffy marshmallows.

MERRY MINCE PIES!

A Christmas classic.

Ingredients

Makes 24 perfect mince pies

260 g unsalted butter, softened

375 g plain flour, plus a sprinkle extra for dusting

125 g caster sugar, plus a little extra for dusting

2 large eggs

800 g jar of mincemeat

Snowcrumb's steps

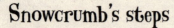

1   Wash your hands really well with
    water and lots of soap.

2   Ask a grown-up to help you cut the
    softened butter into 2-centimetre squares, and then add
    it to a mixing bowl with the flour.

3   Use your fingers to rub the ingredients together until the
    mixture looks like breadcrumbs.

4   Add one egg and the sugar to the bowl, and then mix
    everything together thoroughly.

5   Lightly dust a clean surface with flour, and then tip the
    mixture out on to the floured surface.

6   Fold the mixture until the pastry comes together – try
    not to over-mix it. As soon as it easily forms a ball,
    you're done!

7   Wrap the pastry up in cling film and pop it into the
    fridge to rest for 15 minutes or so.

8   With the permission and help of a grown-up, preheat
    your oven to 220 degrees Celsius and grease a cupcake
    tray (you can use a little butter or a
    light spray of oil).

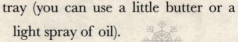

9 Lightly flour your surface again, and roll out the pastry to about 3 millimetres thick. While rolling it out, make sure to turn the pastry 90 degrees between rolling – it will help stop the mixture from sticking to the surface and will make sure you get an even thickness. If the pastry does begin to stick, add a little more flour to the surface.

10 Use a round cutter (about 10 centimetres) to cut out 24 bases and place them gently into your cupcake trays. To make sure the pastry gets right down into the tray, use a little bit of rolled-up pastry to gently push in each base.

11 Push a tablespoon or so of mincemeat into each base.

12 Re-roll your remaining pastry, and use a smaller round cutter (about 7 centimetres) to cut some lids.

13 Crack the second egg into a small dish, then brush the edges of your mince-pie bases with a little egg before placing on the lids. Press the edges of the lids down to seal them to the base.

14 With the help of a grown-up, bake the mince pies for 15–20 minutes – you will know they are ready when they are golden brown and bubbling. **YUM**.

15 Cool the mince pies on a wire rack for a minute or two before removing them from the tray. Once they've cooled slightly, remove them from the tray and place on a wire rack to cool completely.

16 Using a sift, dust the top of the mince pies with a little bit of caster sugar. Enjoy!

At first glance,
the dinosaur had
DEEP-BLUE SCALY SKIN
that was so **reflective** and **shiny**
he could almost have been a
magnificent, translucent
ice sculpture.

But as Santa stepped closer
he saw that the **DINOSAUR'S SKIN**
was a combination of
thousands of rich colours.

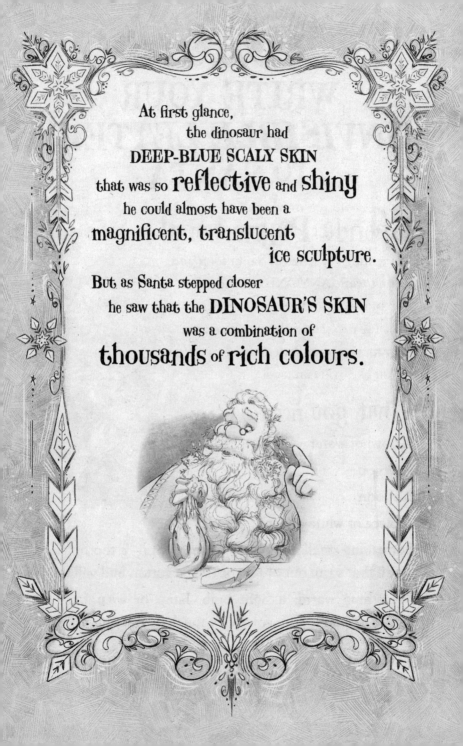

WRITE YOUR *INVISIBLE* LETTER TO SANTA

Brenda Payne here!

I'm writing my letter to Santa soon and I don't want ANYONE to read what I'm putting. So I've got a cheeky trick up my sleeve that's going to help me keep my letter top secret. If you like, you can try it out too!

What you need:

A bowl of water

A lemon

A spoon

A piece of white paper

Something small and pointy to write with – a toothpick, a pen that's run out of ink, or even a cotton bud will do!

Something warm: a light bulb, lamp or even bright sunshine (make sure you don't touch anything hot!)

Dear Santa,

What to do:

1   Ask a grown-up to cut the lemon in half for you, and then squeeze some drops of lemon juice into the bowl of water.

2   Give it a good stir, but be careful not to spill.

3   Dip your toothpick, old pen or cotton bud in the lemony mixture.

4   Use it to write your secret letter to Santa!

5   You can send the letter straight to Santa – he'll know the trick and be able to read it – but if you want to test it out yourself, try holding the paper near warm light and watch your secret message appear!

William went over to Santa
and wrapped his arms round
his **fat-tastic belly**
(which indeed shook when he laughed,
but was more like a
bowl full of thick custard
than jelly).

Hugging Santa was like hugging a
great friendly **polar bear**,
and he was as **warm** as a
fresh mug of
hot chocolate.

MAKE YOUR OWN
WINTER WITCH
SNOW GLOBE

'She's the best-kept Christmas secret of all,' Santa whispered, 'which is surprising, because she is so powerful that Christmas itself would not exist without her. She's older than time itself, yet still as young as tomorrow. She is known only as the Winter Witch.'

The Winter Witch is one of the most magical and mysterious Christmas figures. It's the Winter Witch who freezes time so Santa can travel all round the world before Christmas morning. Here's how you can make your very own Winter Witch snow globe to decorate your bedroom. (Ask a grown-up for permission and help using sharp scissors.)

What you need:

Measuring tape

A clean, watertight glass jar (an empty jam or peanut-butter jar with the label removed and a flat screw-top lid would be perfect)

Scissors

White paper

Felt-tip pens, colouring pencils or paint

Sticky tape

Water

Eco-friendly glitter

What to do:

1 Measure the height and circumference (the distance round the outside) of your jar. Cut out a piece of paper that is the same height as the jar and half the circumference in width.

2 On one side of your paper, use the outline opposite to draw your own Winter Witch. Colour and decorate her using pens, colouring pencils or even paint if you'd like.

3 Wrap your Winter Witch drawing round the jar, with the drawing facing in, and secure it using sticky tape. You should be able to see the Winter Witch by peering through the uncovered side of the jar.

4 Now fill the jar with water and glitter, and screw the lid on tightly.

5 Shake the jar and watch the Winter Witch's magic come to life!

'Nice children can do
NAUGHTY THINGS,
and naughty children can
be **NICE AGAIN,**
which is why everyone deserves
a second chance . . .
ONE SECOND CHANCE
can change a life!'

THE MAGICAL
NORTH POLE

You know that sound when your magical time-travelling ice-cream van crashes into deep snow?

No? You don't have a magical time-travelling ice-cream van?

Oh.

Well, it sounds something like this:

SSSSCCCCHHHWWWOOOOOOOSH!

In about seven pages, a girl named Izzy and her little cousin Benji will hear that sound. But, right

now, they're lying against a tree in Izzy's garden, feeling very, very, VERY hot.

'I'm very, very, VERY hot,' said Izzy.

(I told you.)

Izzy fanned herself with her hand. 'I wish we had a swimming pool!'

Lots of Izzy's friends had gone on exciting summer holidays to places with fancy pools and golden beaches and those cool drinks with colourful umbrellas and swirly-twirly straws. But Izzy's mum and dad had said that they couldn't afford to go away this year, so she and Benji were stuck at home in the garden. And it was **TOO HOT!**

'I'm hotter than a hot dog on the barbecue!' said Izzy.

But Benji didn't laugh.

Izzy looked at her little cousin. Normally on a summer's day Benji would be getting into all sorts of trouble, like climbing a tree and finding himself stuck halfway up. But now he had just flopped on to a branch.

'Do you think it's hot in Greece?' he asked quietly.

Benji was staying with Izzy's family for six months while his mum worked in Greece, digging up old things. (She was an archaeologist, not a dog. Although they both got very excited when they found a bone.)

Izzy knew that Benji must be missing his mum. Luckily, she also knew something that would cheer him up.

'*Do you want to go on an adventure?*' she whispered.

'**YES!**' Benji leapt down from the tree excitedly.

'Mum! We're going to play in the van!' Izzy called.

'OK, Iz!' Mum called back.

I know what you're thinking. Yes, this *is* the magical time-travelling ice-cream van I was telling you about right at the start! Well done!

It was parked on the driveway next to Izzy's garden.

This van used to belong to Izzy's grandpa, and it was very special indeed. Gramps had been an ice-cream man, pouring out the twirliest, twistiest, yummiest ice creams all day long from the machine in the van. After Gramps died, the ice-cream van came to live at Izzy's house and it reminded her of him every time she looked at it. It was exactly the same shade of blue as his warm, twinkly eyes.

But it was **extra-specially special** for another secret reason: it could travel by a strange magic to all kinds of wondrously marvellous, marvellously wondrous places.

I know, right?

AMAZING!

Izzy had discovered this one magical day when she had eaten too much ice cream straight from the machine and got a very bad case of **BRAIN FREEZE!**

The brain freeze was so powerful that it actually **FROZE TIME** – and when Izzy had put the ice-cream van in reverse, it had taken her back to the time of the Ancient Egyptians by accident.

Since then, she had shared the secret with Benji and they had gone on lots of adventures together – forwards, backwards and even sideways in time and space. The best thing was that once they had been on their adventure, the van would bring them back to the very same second that they'd left, so Izzy's mum wouldn't even know they'd gone!

Oh, and they got to eat a **LOT** of ice cream.

Izzy and Benji climbed in and headed straight for the ice-cream machine. Izzy pulled the lever and a swirl of cold, creamy ice cream shot straight out – right into Benji's open mouth.

'**OOOOOOOH!**' said Benji, grabbing his forehead. '**BRAIN FREEZE!**'

'Perfect!' said Izzy. 'My turn!'

As the ice cream poured into her open mouth, she got ready for the chill. It felt as though frosty snowflakes were forming on the inside of her head; as if an icy grip was tightening round her mind. There was a *whoosh* of icy cold air – as if someone had opened a giant freezer. '**AAAAAAAHHHHHH!**' cried Izzy.

Suddenly she was able to relax again. She and Benji glanced round and grinned at the icy layer that had formed over the windows of the van.

'Time to go,' Izzy said, smiling.

They both jumped into their seats and buckled their seat belts. Then Izzy picked up a shiny old alarm clock and twisted its hands round and round. 'I wonder where we'll end up?' she said.

Finally, she turned the keys in the ignition, slammed her foot on the pedals and released the handbrake of the van.

They were off!

There was a sound like ice cubes clinking through pipes, and the van began to move. Faster and faster and faster it went, until the houses around them were just blurs, and the scenery began to change from houses and cars to something

VAST

and cold

and empty

and white.

SSSSCCCCHHHWWWOOOOOOOSH!

The van crashed into deep snow. (Just like I told you it would.)

Izzy and Benji peered out of the window. All they could see was white. Freezing-cold white.

Izzy looked down at her dress and shoes. Benji was wearing shorts and a T-shirt, and was already shivering.

'Well, at least we're not going to be too hot any more,' Izzy said. 'Do you know where we are?'

'I can't tell!' Benji said, looking at the stark white nothing.

Suddenly Izzy spotted something glinting in the snow. She pushed open the van door, which was almost frozen shut with ice, and slowly put one foot down into the crunchy white snow, where it made a deep footprint.

'*Brrrrrr!*' she said. 'Look, Benji, there's something here – it looks a bit like a golden thermometer . . .'

Benji jumped out next to her and stared at the

strange object. It *did* look like a thermometer, with a line of glowing red liquid running up the middle. But what was it doing here? And where were they?

There was something almost magical about this snowy place . . .

Snow?

Magic?

And then Izzy had a brainwave.

'Benji . . .' she said, turning to him with her eyes shining bright. 'You don't think we're at the North Pole, do you?'

Benji's mouth dropped open.

'That means . . .' Izzy continued.

'SANTA!' cried Benji.

And at that very moment . . .

POP!

Benji disappeared! Just like that. In the wink of a blink of an eye. One moment he was right there – a few millimetres from Izzy's face – and the next he was gone!

'Benji?' Izzy called, but her voice drifted on the frozen wind into the distant nothingness.

There was only snow as far as her eyes could see. All of a sudden, a gust of wind *whooshed* past and Izzy thought she heard whispers.

'Benji?' she called again.

Izzy tried to think. Benji must have done something to make himself disappear. But what?

And then she knew.

'SANTA!' she yelled – and the most spectacularly magical thing happened. She didn't disappear like Benji had. Quite the opposite, in fact: EVERYTHING ELSE appeared. And, by EVERYTHING, I mean **EVERYTHING!**

Suddenly Izzy was standing at the entrance to an enormous wooden building. A sign over the doorway said:

Izzy couldn't believe how **grand** it was. As she marvelled at the twisty turrets, the puffing chimneys, the toboggan-run path and the snowflake door knocker, her mouth dropped open in wonder.

'Hi, Izzy!' Benji said, grinning happily. He was now wearing a Christmas jumper with a dinosaur on it, a bobble hat and knitted slippers with curly toes. Izzy looked down and

saw that her clothes had changed too, and she was deliciously warm and cosy in a snowflake coat.

Then Izzy realized that she and Benji were not alone. They were surrounded by a crowd of creatures. Small, strange, magical creatures! Even though Izzy had never seen one before, she knew at once that these small creatures were **ELVES!**

'Hello, elves!' she said.

The elves all backed off, looking nervous. Then one by one they popped out again, looking frightened and cross, before all of a sudden they started singing!

'Some kids are here! Some kids, it's true!
Oh, what are we poor elves to do?
They've seen our secret hiding spot
And everything has gone to pot!
We could not leave them there to freeze –
We heard them yelling on the breeze –
And so we brought them here today
But what will Santa think and say?
He'll soon be back from holiday!
He'll land here in his great red sleigh!
Quick! Turn around! Move out the way!
Santa's back, hip hip hooray!'

The elves stopped singing and stood back. Izzy and Benji spun round to see a gigantic red sleigh appear out of thin air above them, and circle down very fast towards where they were standing. The sleigh was even more incredible than Izzy could ever have dreamt it to be.

Shimmeringly shiny, ridonkulously red and monstrously massive!

But that wasn't the most wonderful thing about it. Most wonderful, Izzy thought, were the powerful creatures pulling it. She counted eight in total, striding through the air side by side, their antlers gleaming. The flying reindeer!

'Whoa, whoa, whoa!' cried a deep, booming voice from overhead as the sleigh swooped round them and then touched down with a smooth *swish* along the snow. That's when Izzy first saw him. She couldn't believe her eyes. It was really him. Actually. Genuinely. One hundred per cent authentically. The real deal.

'SANTA!' Benji yelled again.

Santa pulled hard on the reins and the sleigh came to a stop directly in front of Izzy, Benji and the crowd of tiny elves that had gathered to greet him.

The elves rushed forward, cheering and screaming like crazed fans at a rock concert, but Izzy still had a perfect view of Santa as the elves were only half Benji's height! The mind-blowingly massive man stepped down from his sleigh. He wasn't wearing his famous red suit but blue shorts and a colourful Hawaiian shirt decorated with palm trees. On his head was a yellow baseball cap bearing the words HO HO HOLIDAY!

(That's right. Even Santa likes to have a summer holiday!)

Apart from his clothes, Santa looked every bit the jolly, happy man you would expect. But Izzy was worried. The elf song had made her feel naughty, as if she and Benji shouldn't be there! What would Santa do? What would he say?

She was about to find out.

Santa spotted something out of place – Izzy and Benji!

'What the crackers is *this*?' he asked, completely confuddled. He bounced straight over to where they were squished in the centre of a crowd of elves, and stood, towering impressively, over them. 'You're a little tall for an elf!' he said as Benji giggled delightedly. '*Why*, you're not an elf at all! Nor a skating snowman, nor a forest fairy, nor a reindeer!' He glanced at Izzy. 'Tell me, are you a mountain troll? Yes, I've heard of lost, wandering trolls before, but never seen one. How fascinating!' He rubbed his hands together excitedly.

'We're not **TROLLS!**' Izzy laughed.

Santa paused and scratched his beard thoughtfully.

'No . . . of course you're not! Wait . . . don't tell me . . . you're a . . . **BALD YETI!** *Yes!* That's it. How peculiar!'

'No!' Benji giggled. 'We're not one of those either!'

'Hmmm, not a troll and not a bald yeti, eh? Don't tell me! I'm thinking, I'm thinking, I'm thinking . . . Oh, what a fun guessing game this is!'

Santa did a little hop and a skip and walked round Izzy and Benji, inspecting them.

'Santa!' Benji said politely. 'I'm not a troll or a yeti. **I'M JUST A BOY!**'

There was a sudden rumble of whispers from the surrounding elves.

'*Just* a boy?' Santa bellowed in his mighty voice.

Izzy pulled Benji close. She was unsure if Santa was jolly happy or jolly angry.

'JUST a boy?' he repeated, and looked around at his elves. Then all of a sudden Santa seemed to find something completely hilarious.

'**HA-HA-HA! HO-HO-HO!**' He boomed an enormous laugh that made his belly ripple and wobble. 'There's no such thing as JUST a boy! Allow me to explain. You see, up here we have all sorts of wonderfully magical creatures. But there's something we don't have – the most magical creatures in all the world . . .'

Izzy and Benji didn't have a clue what they could be.

'Children!' Santa said with a smile.

'*Children?*' Izzy said. 'Children aren't magic. I'm a child and I'm not magic at all!'

All the elves giggled and Santa smiled knowingly.

'Oh, but you are! You really, truly are. You just don't know it! You can create impossible worlds in your imagination that don't really exist. *That* is magic. Because you can only see the best in people, the best in the world, in life. *That* is magic. Because you understand the importance of silliness, the importance of fun, of laughing and playing, which grown-ups have forgotten. *That* is magic. But, most of all, because you believe, without question, in the impossible. Without needing proof. Without hesitation. *That* is magic.'

Izzy couldn't believe what she was hearing. She could do all those things and she hadn't even realized that they were magic!

'Aha! And, speaking of belief, I see you have something of mine.' Santa pointed to the strange golden thermometer in Izzy's hand.

'Oh, is it yours, Santa? I found it in the snow!' Izzy explained, handing it over to the ginormous man.

'Well, butter my crumpets, what a stroke of luck! This is my **beliefometer**. I lost it a little while ago, when I was out making a snow angel in a fresh mound of snow. It must have fallen out of my pocket! It's a very special instrument that allows me and my elves to measure belief.' He pointed to the glowing red line and beamed. 'And it looks like the children of the world still have plenty of belief! That's jolly good news. You see, belief is the reason I am able to exist . . .

Izzy and Benji.'

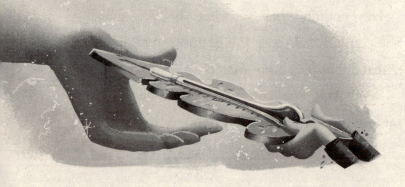

At the mention of their names, Izzy couldn't help but notice that all the elves started whispering among themselves again.

'How do you know our names?' she asked. 'We haven't told you them.'

'Well, it took me a moment to realize who you were. I didn't expect to see any youngsters at the North Pole, you see. We haven't had children here for a very long time,' said Santa thoughtfully. 'But, now that you're here, why don't you come inside?' He opened his arms and stepped up to the enormous wooden doors of his Snow Ranch. 'Let's go!'

Santa led Izzy and Benji through some smaller, more sensibly sized doors that were cut into the ridiculously large doors and they entered the grandest entrance hall you could possibly imagine.

You want to try? Go ahead!

Imagine

GIGANTIC,

quadruple-height ceilings . . .

Keep going . . .

A little taller than that.

Whoa!

Stop!

That's just silly! Bring them down a tad . . .

There! That looks about right.

The floors were made of huge slabs of Christmas-tree pine that were as warm as a cup of tea under your feet. That's because the underfloor-heating system used actual English breakfast tea to heat the pipes.

The air smelt of fresh *vaninnamon* (that's vanilla and cinnamon mixed together), and the sounds of carols and pointless family bickering – the true sounds of Christmas – echoed from somewhere in the distance. Izzy and Benji couldn't believe their eyes, ears or noses.

'Come in, come in! Welcome to my home.' Santa grinned as he spun round merrily with his arms wide.

'This place is amazing!' Benji gasped.

'We have everything you could possibly imagine, and a few things you probably can't,' Santa said with a chuckle, as he skipped down the wooden hallway of his supersized log cabin, its walls decorated with colourful drawings from children around the world. He did a little cartwheel and went into a forward roll, then pushed open heavy double doors leading to what looked like a library.

'Look at all the books!' Izzy cried.

'These aren't books – these are the lists,' Santa said, running his fingers over the ancient spines of thick tomes that lined every wall.

'You mean, *the* Nice List?' Izzy asked.

'And the Naughty one,' Santa replied, pointing to the opposite wall, which housed an equally daunting number of books.

Izzy laughed as Benji gave a little shudder. 'I hope I'm never on the Naughty List!' he said.

Santa led them to the library fireplace, where there were two big chairs next to a roaring fire. Santa sat on one and Izzy and Benji sat together on the other (the chairs were Santa-sized, so there was more than enough room for them both).

'Ah, it's good to be home, even though I did enjoy getting a bit of sunshine!' Santa said.

Izzy closed her eyes. Suddenly glorious music filled the air. A **gramophone** on a table next to the fire had burst into life on its own and was playing a beautiful song. Izzy opened her eyes and was surprised to see Santa and the elves all staring up at something. Something above her head.

'What is it?' Benji said, hopping about. 'I can't see!'

Izzy looked up, and what she saw completely took her breath away. The greens and blues, purples and yellows of the Northern Lights had been wondrously woven into a shape in the starry sky over the North Pole – it was her mum, her dad and Benji, and everyone was on holiday, having fun! Izzy could hardly take it all in.

Then, all of a sudden, the lights and colours started swaying and swirling around to the sound pouring from the gramophone, and in

the sky Benji ran up to another figure and leapt
into her arms. And there was Benji with his mum.
Izzy thought how much her little cousin was
missing his mum, and suddenly she knew exactly
what she wanted.

Santa winked. 'It will be done,' he promised.

'Thank you, Santa,' she said with a smile.

As the Northern Lights flickered overhead, Izzy
felt that it was time to go home.

'Come on,' she said to Benji.

'But we just got here!' Benji complained.

'OH!' all the elves sighed.

Two of them put their arms round Benji.

'Don't say you're leaving, no, not yet!
Can't we keep him as our pet?'

Izzy smiled. She would
have loved to stay and explore
more of the magical North
Pole. But she could feel her
brain freeze beginning to
wear off – and indeed
Santa and the elves had
A LOT of work to do.

'We've got to go,' she said. 'Besides, I want my
present!'

'What did you ask for?' Benji asked.

'Wait and see!' Izzy told him, smiling secretively.

Before they left, Santa gave them each a big
hug. It was like falling into the squishiest armchair
ever, one that was so deep you almost got stuck.
Then they ran through the snow back to the van,
all the elves following them and waving madly.

As they buckled their seat belts, Izzy stared at the amazing sight of the ranch, Santa and the elves for a moment longer before she started the engine. She never wanted to forget this place! They waved and the whole ranch, with Santa and the elves waving back at them, disappeared.

Their Christmas outfits faded away, leaving them in their summer clothes. But then the cosy clothes reappeared, neatly folded on the van's dashboard, with a note that said: **FOR YOUR NEXT CHILLY ADVENTURE.**

They both sighed as the van whisked them off and they landed with a bump back in Izzy's driveway.

'That was just . . . magic!' Benji said happily. 'I can't wait for Christmas now!'

Izzy threw open the van's doors and the sunshine poured over them like melted butter. 'Neither can I, but right now let's enjoy the summer!' She grinned. It was nice to be warm again!

'IZZY! BENJI!'

Izzy's mum came running out of the house with an excited shriek, flapping something in the air. It looked like a letter. 'Guess what? I entered a competition, and I've won a family holiday to Greece! I can't believe it! We can go and visit your mum, Benji!'

Benji's eyes went wide. 'I can see Mum?' he gasped – then looked at Izzy. 'Your present! That's what you asked for!' He gave Izzy a tight hug and whispered, 'Thank you, Iz.'

'Oh, and there's something else that arrived for you two,' Mum said, pointing to the back garden.

'What did you get? It'd better not be a dinosaur,' Izzy warned.

Benji gave an excited grin and they both ran to the back garden. There was an enormous paddling pool – and it was shaped like a *dinosaur!* Dad was filling it up with a hosepipe.

'We don't know who sent it to you. It just came with this postcard,' Mum said, looking confused.

Izzy and Benji took the postcard. On one side there was a picture of the swirling, swooping Northern Lights. On the other side it read: *Izzy and Benji, have a brilliant summer holiday!*

'You said you wanted to go swimming,' Benji said, shrugging as Izzy hugged him.

They ran upstairs to get changed into their swimsuits. Another adventure was over, but Izzy and Benji's summer fun had just begun!

THE END

THE CHRISTMAS PUDDING PUZZLES

Put your brain to the test with these Christmas head-scratchers. You'll find the answers at the back of the book (but no peeping, unless you want to end up on the Naughty List).

CHRISTMAS WORD SCRAMBLE

The Christmasaurus has got in a spin and muddled up these Christmas words! Can you work them out?

1 sehliġ

2 elaġn

3 reet

4 corasl

5 remry

6 timltoese

7 ylihado

8 knġstcoi

FESTIVE RIDDLES

Can you identify these Christmassy
things from their descriptions?

1 We're Santa's little helpers, and
   we're loved by girls and boys.
   All throughout the year, we work hard making toys.
   Who are we?

2 My body is round. I have a carrot for a nose.
   I love to relax in the cold, from my head to my toes.
   What am I?

3 I'm a colourful metallic strip, as shiny as can be.
   Hung all round your Christmas tree is where you'll
   find me.
   What am I?

4 We're four-legged friends, pullers of Santa's sleigh.
   If you're on the Nice List, we just might come your way!
   What are we?

WILLIAM'S WORD SEARCH

Can you find these Christmas characters hidden in the word search?

BOB

BRENDA

CHRISTMASAURUS

ELLA

MARVIN

PAMELA

RONNIE

SANTA

SPROUT

SPUDCHEEK

TRULY

UTTERLY

C	Q	R	A	E	L	L	A	A	I	U	R	M	O
M	H	T	P	R	T	H	N	E	M	I	B	M	S
N	T	R	O	N	N	I	E	X	E	O	E	E	P
C	Y	U	I	E	R	B	G	V	D	A	N	T	U
P	A	L	E	S	A	N	T	A	B	O	B	A	D
A	S	Y	F	P	T	A	E	R	R	A	Y	L	C
M	E	R	V	R	I	M	I	D	E	R	H	P	H
E	E	A	S	O	S	A	A	N	N	L	H	O	E
L	C	M	T	U	P	R	T	S	D	O	P	H	E
A	V	R	B	T	J	V	A	A	A	B	P	C	K
A	U	T	A	E	U	I	E	T	I	U	L	R	L
I	J	I	M	G	E	N	R	G	S	B	R	T	O
S	H	R	T	I	E	Y	L	R	E	T	T	U	J
B	C	A	S	K	T	P	A	T	R	Y	L	V	S

SPOT THE DINO-DIFFERENCE!

Can you find the five differences between these two pictures?

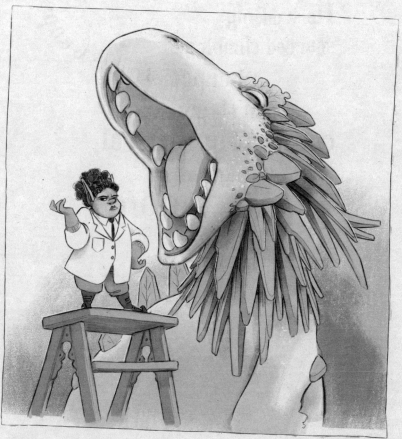

The Christmasaurus let out
a happy **roar**
of excitement.
He was almost home.
He suddenly
started climbing,
steeper and steeper
until they were
completely vertical,
facing the
moon!

Jingle Jokes

Test out these belly-wobblers on your family and friends!

Why does everyone love
FROSTY THE SNOWMAN?
Because he's cool.

Why did the **CHRISTMAS TREE**
go to the **BARBER?**
It needed a trim!

What do you call an ELF
wearing EARMUFFS?
Anything you fancy –
they can't hear you anyway!

What do you get when you
cross a CHRISTMAS TREE
with an APPLE?
A pineapple!

What do SNOWMEN eat
for BREAKFAST?
Snowflakes!

What happens if you EAT
Christmas decorations?
You get tinselitis.

What do you call SANTA
when he stops moving?
Santa Pause.

What FALLS but
never gets HURT?
Snow!

CHRISTMAS AROUND THE WORLD

Ho, Ho, Ho!

It's Santa here – the real deal, the Big Bauble, the magical man himself! How the jingle are you?

When I whizz around in my sleigh delivering presents to all the children around the world, I get to see lots and lots and **LOTS** of different Christmas traditions – some of which may surprise you!

- The first **advent calendar** was made in Germany in 1851. Tinsel was also invented in Germany, in 1610, and the first garland was made of **REAL silver!**

- In Italy, children write letters to **Babbo Natale** (that's me!) to tell him that they've been good throughout the year. The main day for giving presents is Twelfth Night, or 6 January (but it's the evening of 5 January for some people) – and legend has it that those gifts are brought by a **good witch** called La Befana. La Befana brings sweet treats and other goodies in the middle of the night, and then sweeps the floor with her famous broom before leaving! How kind! I wonder if she's related to the Winter Witch . . . ?

- An estimated **3.6 million** Japanese families get their holiday meal from none other than Kentucky Fried Chicken on Christmas Day!

- On Christmas Eve in Sweden, more than half the country sit down to watch a Disney Christmas special on TV.

- In China, only one in every one hundred people celebrates Christmas. It's a light-hearted day, when people often go ice skating, to the cinema, out shopping or to the **karaoke bar** for a good old sing-a-thon!

- In Brazil, some children leave a sock near a window. If **Papai Noel** (that's me too!) finds it, he will swap it for a present. (Just make sure it's not a **stinky** sock, please!)

- **Christmas lanterns** have become a special tradition in the Philippines. They're called parols and are usually made from bamboo and Japanese paper. Most often the parols come in the shape of a five-pointed star.

- In both Egypt and Ethiopia, people celebrate Christmas not on 25 December but on 7 January! **Fancy that!**

- In the Gambia, people celebrate Christmas with an enormous parade, with large lanterns and handmade bamboo-and-paper boats set on wheels. There's music and a **huge celebration** throughout the day.

- Christmas Day in sunny Australia often involves going to the beach with family for a celebratory barbecue – or, as Australians usually call it, a 'barbie'. I'll take **three hot dogs**, please!

- In Ghana, December is not just a time to celebrate Christmas; it's also a celebration of **CHOCOLATE!** This is because December marks the beginning of the cacao (the bean that makes chocolate) harvest. **YUM!**

- In France, the most important Christmas meal is called réveillon, and it happens late on Christmas Eve or very early on Christmas Day, after people return home from Midnight Mass. A special chocolate log cake, called a **bûche de Noël**, is often eaten.

- The main Christmas meal happens on Christmas Eve in the Czech Republic too, but it's traditional to eat fish soup, followed by fried fish and potato salad.

- Norway gives the UK a very special Christmas present every year: an **enormous Christmas tree**. It's a thank you for the help that the UK gave to Norway during the Second World War, and it stands in Trafalgar Square in London.

- They don't just have one Santa Claus in Iceland; they are lucky enough to have thirteen! **The Yule Lads**, as they're called, each take turns visiting children on the thirteen nights leading up to Christmas. Gamlárskvöld – New Year's Eve – is a very special and magical night in Iceland, when all sorts of strange things take place. Legend has it that cows can talk, seals take on human form, and the **elves** move house! In fact, I'd better check my own elves have stayed put.

DINO-RRIFIC DECORATIONS

Here's the Christmasaurus's favourite fun way to make fantastic decorations for the Christmas tree. Once, the Christmasaurus actually tried to eat these and his dino-tummy was very unhappy afterwards. These decorations are definitely just for looking at and not for chomping on! Just like Snowcrumb's recipes, it's best to ask a grown-up for permission and help, especially when using a hot oven.

What you need:

Makes 10–12 decorations

A baking tray

Greaseproof paper

250 g plain flour, with a little extra for dusting

125 g table salt (fine salt is best)

A bowl

125 g water

A wooden spoon

A rolling pin

Biscuit cutters (any shape will do, but the more
  Christmassy, the better!)

A pencil or pen

Felt-tip pens, paints or eco-friendly glitter for
  decoration

String or thin ribbon

What to do:

1   With the permission and help of a grown-up, preheat the oven to its lowest setting and line a baking tray with greaseproof paper.

2   Mix the flour and salt in a bowl. Add the water gradually, and stir with a wooden spoon until the mixture comes together into a ball.

3   Lightly dust a clean surface with flour, and then move the dough ball to the floured surface. Using your rolling pin, roll the dough out flat until it's around a centimetre thick. (If you don't have a rolling pin, you can always use your hands to press the dough flat.)

4   Press biscuit cutters into the dough to cut out shapes.

5   With the tip of a pencil or pen, poke a small hole in the top of each shape.

6   Carefully place your shapes on to the baking tray.

7   With the help of a grown-up, bake at your oven's lowest heat for three hours, or until solid. Remove from the oven and leave to cool completely.

8 Now for the fun part! Once your shapes have cooled, you can paint and decorate them any way you like. Paint that has a sprinkling of glitter looks dino-tastic!

9 When your decorations are completely dry, push a piece of string or ribbon through the hole at the top of each shape and tie in a knot. Now your homemade decorations are ready to hang on your Christmas tree!

WRITE YOUR OWN CHRISTMAS POEM

'I heard a noise on the rooftop!
It made my heart go jump!
The stomp of boots
And the clop of hooves
Went clippety, clippety, clump!'

The elves love to speak in rhyme as much as they can. Here's everything you'll need to write your very own rhyming Christmas poem!

1. Pen 2. Paper 3. Your imagination

Have a look at the word bank opposite and see if you can pick some Christmassy words to continue the poems we have started for you here. If you'd like to write a non-rhyming poem instead, you can do that too!

Word Bank

ADVENT   ANGEL   BELLS   BELLY

BRIGHT   CANDY CANE   CAROL

CHILLY   CHEERFUL   COAL

CRANBERRIES   CRUMPETS   DARK

ELF   FESTIVE   FLIGHT   FROSTY

GIFT   GLOW   HOLLY   HARK

ICICLE   JINGLE   JELLY   JOLLY

MISTLETOE   PAWS   PLEASANT

PRESENT   REINDEER   RHYME

SANTA   SMELLS   SNOW   SNOWBALL

SNOWMAN   TIME   TINSEL   TWINKLE

1. It was a snowy, icy Christmas night . . .

2. A dinosaur came one Christmas time . . .

3. 'LOOK IN THE SKY!' called Santa Claus . . .

119

TOM'S TOP TEN THINGS ABOUT CHRISTMAS

(NARROWED DOWN FROM 1,000)

 1 **The music!** Christmas songs rule. Full stop. Is it just me, or is 'I Wish It Could Be Christmas Everyday' the most relatable lyric of all time? Oh . . . it is just me.

 2 **Food, and lots of it.** I love everything about festive food. Even food I don't like – give it a Christmassy name and some magical packaging and it's in my shopping basket. Rename mixed nuts 'The Festive Mix' and SOLD! What even is a figgy pudding? Who cares! Nom nom nom.

Christmas movies. We all know the ones I'm talking about. *Elf*, *Home Alone* (1 AND 2), *White Christmas*, *Miracle on 34th Street* . . . The list goes on and on and on. And let's not forget *Die Hard*.

The Snowman. *The Snowman* deserves to be listed on its own. I'm talking about both the book and the film. I have loved it since I was a little boy, and watching my son Buzz fall in love with it at Christmas and asking me to lift him up so that he could fly like the Snowman was an incredible moment.

TV adverts. I know what you're thinking. 'Who in their right mind gets excited about TV adverts?' ME, that's who. Companies have been majorly upping their game these last few years. Monty the penguin was quite possibly the best ad of all time. I cried ugly tears.

6 Christmas Eve.

I don't care that I'm in my thirties – I still get excited on Christmas Eve. It's by far the most magical night of the year and I remember exactly how it felt when I was a kid. I'm loving the fact that I get to experience it again through my own kids now.

7 **Friends and family.** It goes without saying that it's the time of year you make that extra effort to see those people you don't see as often as you should. When I think back on all my favourite Christmas memories, they're filled with my family or my friends – so I guess they deserve to be on the list.

8 **Christmas dinner.** I'm listing this separately from the other festive food because this meal is the ultimate. I've been in charge of the big meal for the last few years and, although I had a disaster with the gravy a while back, on the whole I think I've got pretty good at it. Of course you have to make a few practice meals in the weeks/months leading up to it, just to be safe.

9 **Street lights.** Our local high street has used the same Christmas lights for at least the last ten years, probably longer. They aren't anything special really, but that doesn't stop them from filling me with Christmas awesomeness the moment they are switched on. I always drive the long way home in December just so I get to see them. One year they tested them out in the summer in the middle of the night and I managed to get a sneaky look at them early. I was happy.

10 Last but not least, fake Christmas trees.

Wait – did I just say fake? Yes, you read that right. Believe it or not, I'm pretty sure I have a mild allergy to Christmas trees (yes, that makes me very sad). It doesn't affect me badly, but having a real one in the house for over a month has caused me some serious issues. So I am REALLY grateful to whoever thought up the idea of fake Christmas trees. We've had the same one for as long as we have lived in our house and, even though it's looking a little shabby these days, it wouldn't be Christmas without it. (I still risk the allergy and sometimes have a small real tree in the kitchen . . . Can't help myself!)

ANSWERS

CHRISTMAS WORD SCRAMBLE

1 sleigh   5 merry

2 angel   6 mistletoe

3 tree   7 holiday

4 carols   8 stocking

FESTIVE RIDDLES

1 We are elves.

2 I am a snowman.

3 I am tinsel.

4 We are reindeer.

WILLIAM'S WORD SEARCH

SPOT THE DINO-DIFFERENCE!

INTRO

I'm **GEORGE**.
George Racket.
I play **BASS GUITAR**.

And this is **NEILA**.
She plays **GUITAR**.

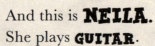

This is **BASH**.
He plays the **DRUMS**.

And together we are . . .

THE EARTHLINGS!

The <u>best</u> band
in the universe!

We never meant to become intergalactic rock stars,
or to save the world from being pulverized by evil
aliens using only the power of music. It just sort of . . .
happened.

We weren't always super-awesome, guitar-shredding,
drum-soloing music legends either.

In fact, before we were unexpectedly beamed up into outer space, we were actually pretty awful. And I don't mean just a bad band.

We TOTALLY SUCKED!

I'm serious. Our own parents couldn't even pretend to like the noises that leaked out of our garage – the place where we rehearsed every day after school. And parents are supposed to like *everything* their kids do!

We were so bad that our neighbours moved house. And our neighbours' neighbours. And even their neighbours too!

I bet you're thinking, *How did the worst band in the world become the best band in the universe?*

I guess it all began on the day I started writing my own songs and decided to put them all down in a book.

This book, in fact. The book you're about to read.

So turn the volume up to infinity, and get ready to rock 'n' roll out of this solar system.

It's time for lift-off!

TRACK 1

THE BOOK OF ROCK

NAME: GEORGE RACKET

SUBJECT: ~~Science~~ ROCK 'N' ROLL

TEACHER: ~~Mr Lloyd~~ LIFE!

Welcome to the book that's going to change my life.

That's right. This is **THE** book. The book that's going to turn me, George Racket, from the ordinary, slightly-shorter-than-average ten-year-old into a super-awesome international

ROCK STAR!

OK, I know on the outside this book looks like a normal school exercise book . . . and it kind of is. (I 'borrowed' it from the classroom supply cupboard.) But that's just a clever disguise.

It will be on these very pages, where boring equations and snore-fest theories would normally be written, that I shall write my masterpiece of musical awesomeness!

Normal exercise book

THIS – my first-ever *songbook*!

No, hang on. *Songbook* sounds a bit rubbish.

My first-ever *music book*?

Nope.

Wait. I've got it . . .

MY BOOK OF ROCK!

To be honest, I'm not quite sure how to write songs yet, but my music idol, rock-legend Max Riff, lead singer of the Comets, once said:

> ### THE GREATEST SONGS ARE BASED ON REAL EXPERIENCES, DUDE. LIVE. WRITE. ROCK!

Live. Write. Rock! If that worked for Max Riff, it can work for George Racket! So I've decided I should start writing down everything that happens to me.

That's right. **EVERYTHING**.

Starting now!

OK, let's see . . . I'm in the most **BORING** lesson at Greyville School: Mr Lloyd's science class. He's got his usual white lab coat on and his hair looks like a science experiment itself.

I don't think he really needs to
wear a lab coat in class. It'd be a bit
like our history teacher, Mr Bygone,
dressing like Henry VIII. Or our
maths teacher, Mrs Spearing, dressing like a calculator.
Or Ms Feather, our art teacher, dressing like a pencil.

Mr Lloyd is writing something on the board.
Something about space – but no one is listening,
because there's something **WAY** more interesting
going on . . .